JACK
and the
BEANSTALK

Illustrated by
ANNE SCHEU BERRY

RAND McNALLY & COMPANY • CHICAGO

ONCE UPON A TIME there was a poor
widow who had an only son, named
Jack. He was good-natured and affec-
tionate but lazy. As time went on, the
widow grew poorer and poorer until she
had nothing left but her cow. And all the
time, it seemed, Jack grew lazier and
lazier.

One day Jack's mother said to him: "Tomorrow you must take the cow to market. The more money you get for her the better for us, for we have nothing left to live on."

Next morning Jack got up earlier than usual, hung a horn around his shoulder, and started out with the cow. He was very happy at having such an important errand. On the way to market he met a queer little old man.

"Good-morning, my lad," said the queer little old man. "Where may you be going with that fine cow?"

"To market," replied Jack.

"And what may you be going to market for?" asked the queer little old man.

"To sell the cow," said Jack.

"As if you had wit enough to sell cows!" chuckled the queer little old man. "A bit of a lad that doesn't even know how many beans make five!"

"Two in each hand and one in your mouth," answered Jack, with a quickness that would have made his mother proud.

"Oho!" laughed the queer little old man. "Oho! Since you know beans, suppose you look at these," and he held out his hand, filled with sunrise-colored, sunset-colored, rainbow-colored beans. "I'll give you all these for your cow."

"That would be a good bargain,"

thought Jack; so he traded the cow for the beans and hurried home.

"Look, Mother," he said gleefully, as he poured the beans into her lap, "I got all these pretty beans for the cow."

"You stupid boy!" she cried. "Now we shall have to starve." And she flung the beans out of the open window.

The next morning Jack woke early. He ran into the garden and found a beanstalk! had sprung up during the night from the beans his mother had thrown away, and had grown so quickly its top was out of sight.

Jack began to climb, and he climbed and he climbed until he reached the top. He stepped off into the sky and walked on and on until he met a beautiful woman with a face like a star.

Now the lady was a fairy and she knew what Jack was thinking and answered him without his asking any questions.

She told Jack he was in a country that belonged to a wicked Giant. This Giant had killed Jack's father and stolen all his gold and precious things. Jack had been only a baby at that time and could not remember, and his mother had been too sad ever to talk to him about it. But that was why she was poor.

"If you and your mother are ever to be happy again," said the fairy, "you must punish that Giant. It will not be an easy thing to do, but you will succeed if you are brave."

The fairy whispered in Jack's ear for a minute, telling him what to do. Then she left him and Jack walked on and on and on.

Toward evening he came to the door of a castle. He blew his horn, and a woman as broad as she was tall opened the door. "I am very tired and hungry," said Jack politely. "Can you give me supper and a night's lodging?"

"You little know, my poor lad, what you ask," sighed the square woman. "My

husband is a Giant and eats people. He would be sure to find you and eat you for his supper. No, no, it would never do!" And she shut the door.

But Jack was too tired to go another step, so he blew his horn again, and when the Giant's wife came to the door he begged her to let him in. The Giant's

wife began to cry, but at last she led Jack
softly into the castle. She took him past
many large rooms. Then they came to the
kitchen, and soon Jack was enjoying a
good meal and quite forgetting to be
afraid. But before he had finished there
came a *thump, thump, thump* of heavy

feet, and in less than no time the Giant's wife had popped Jack into the great oven to hide.

The Giant walked in sniffing the air. "I smell boy," he thundered.

"You are dreaming," laughed his wife, "but there is something better than dreams in this dish." So the Giant stopped sniffing and sat down to supper.

Through a hole in the oven Jack peeped out and watched the Giant eat. And how he did gobble! It seemed to Jack that no one, not even a Giant, could possibly eat so much. When all the dishes were empty, the Giant bade his wife: "Bring me my hen."

She brought a much-ruffled hen and put it on the table.

"Lay," shouted the Giant, and the hen laid a golden egg.

"Another," roared the Giant, and the hen, though she had not finished cackling over the first, laid another golden egg.

Again and again the Giant shouted his orders in a voice of thunder, and again and again the hen obeyed, till there were twelve golden eggs on the table. Then the Giant went to sleep and snored so loud that the house shook.

When the biggest snore of all had shaken Jack out of the oven, he seized the hen and ran off as fast as he could. On and on and on he ran, until he reached the top of the beanstalk. He climbed quickly down and carried the wonderful hen, still cackling, to his mother. Day after day the hen laid its golden eggs, and by selling them Jack and his mother might have lived in luxury all their lives.

But Jack kept thinking about that wicked Giant who had killed his father, and of the fairy's command. So one day he climbed the beanstalk again. When he reached the top he stepped off, followed the same path as before, and arrived at the Giant's castle. This time he had

dressed himself to look like a very differ-
ent person, as he did not want the Giant's
wife to know him. And, sure enough,
when the square woman came to the
door, she did not recognize the lad she
had hidden in the oven.

"Please," said Jack, "can you give me
food and a place to rest? I am hungry and
tired."

"You can't get in here," answered the Giant's wife. "Once before I took in a tired and hungry young runaway, and he stole my husband's precious hen that lays golden eggs."

But Jack talked to the Giant's wife so pleasantly that she thought it would be unkind to grudge him a meal. So she let him come in. After Jack had a good supper, the Giant's wife hid him in a big cupboard. And it was none too soon, either, for in stalked the Giant, *thump, thump, thump,* sniffing the air. "I smell boy," he bellowed.

"Stuff and nonsense," said his wife, as she placed his supper on the table.

After supper the Giant roared, "Fetch me my moneybags."

His wife brought two heavy bags, one full of silver and one full of gold; and

Jack, peeping out of the cupboard, said to himself: "Those were my father's moneybags." The Giant emptied the money out of the bags, counted it over and over again, and then put it back. Very soon he was fast asleep.

As soon as Jack heard the Giant's loud snores, he stole out of the cupboard, snatched up the bags, and ran off as fast as he could. On and on he ran until he reached the top of the beanstalk. Then he dropped the moneybags into his mother's garden and climbed quickly down the beanstalk after them.

Jack and his mother were now as rich as the King and Queen, yet Jack felt that the Giant had not been punished enough. But it was some time before he dared to climb again to the land at the top of the beanstalk.

At last, however, Jack made up his mind to disguise himself like a chimney sweep and see if he could persuade the Giant's wife to let him in once more. He climbed the beanstalk, followed the same path, and came to the castle door. The square woman did not know him, and he begged her for a night's lodging.

"No, no, no," she said.

But Jack begged and begged, and at

last the Giant's wife took pity on him, gave him his supper, and then turned over an empty kettle and hid him under it. Soon the Giant thumped in, sniffing the air, and roared out: "I smell boy."

"Boy?" laughed his wife. "You are always smelling boy."

After supper the Giant shouted: "Fetch me my harp."

"Play!" commanded the Giant, and the harp began to play all by itself. Such lovely tunes Jack had never heard. It played and played until it played the Giant to sleep, and his snores drowned the sweet music. Then Jack jumped out from under the kettle and seized the harp. But no sooner had he slung it up over his shoulder than it cried out: "Master, Master!"

Jack was frightened and ran for his life toward the top of the beanstalk. He could hear the Giant running behind him, *thump, thump, thump,* but the Giant was so heavy he could not run very fast. Jack reached the top of the beanstalk and slid down it as quick as lightning, calling out as he went: "Mother, Mother! The ax, the ax!"

Jack's mother, holding out the ax, met